WISHFUL

THINKING

Daniel's Tale

VICTORIOUS
BUY

Christian James

Printed in the United States of America

First Printing: May 2024

Victorious Buy

ISBN 9798324997670

To mom and dad,

my guiding stars,

whose love illuminates every page and

whose support crafts the spine of this work;

And to God,

the North Star,

without Whose guidance we'd all be lost.

WISHFUL

THINKING

Daniel's Tale

Book #1
Wishful Thinking Series

Written by
Christian James

CHAPTER 1
COACH REYNOLDS

It was another quiet morning in Riverdale as Daniel Fisher's alarm woke him up for school. In the back of his mind, the afterglow of the dream he'd been having still swirled around in a confusing fog. Had he really been kicking soccer balls that split open like chocolate Easter eggs, causing his teammates to yell at him? When did soccer balls start doing that? Seconds ago?

He lay in bed, listening to the soft chirping of birds and the sound of the microwave coming from the kitchen, when he remembered that today was Monday. He shook off the nonsensical dream from his mind with the help of a much more pressing realization: he'd have to see coach Reynolds first thing in the morning.

Daniel let out an irritated groan, lazily waddling out of his room over to the breakfast table. His messy chestnut-brown hairs were pointing in every direction possible.

"Morning sunshine! What's that face for?" asked his mom, smiling at him as she grabbed a milk carton from the fridge.

"Morning, mom. It's just... I have P.E. today." Daniel replied. He gave her a kiss, then walked over to hug his dad, who looked up from the book he was reading.

"What's wrong with P.E.?" he asked, returning his son's hug. Daniel looked away as he thought about how to respond.

You see, he had always loved P.E. In fact, he was an active boy—and had been throughout his childhood. His dad raised him to love the outdoors, especially if it involved kicking a soccer ball around.

"Coach Reynolds just doesn't like me—for no reason," Daniel finally answered, though with a half-truth. The whole truth, which he knew very well, was that Mr. Reynolds took issue with Daniel's recent lazy streak. He had developed a tendency to ignore directions and take shortcuts anywhere he could, naturally driving the discipline-focused coach mad.

Like that time they were supposed to run laps around the basketball court's perimeter, and Daniel ran across the corners whenever he thought coach Reynolds wasn't looking. He'd gotten two hours of detention for that little "joke," as he'd tried to explain it.

"Also, it makes me tired," Daniel added, now hoping to change the subject. Raising his eyebrows, Mr. Fisher took a sip of his coffee.

"You shouldn't be getting *that* tired at your age, Danny. Besides, I thought you were going to try out for the soccer team next month?"

"Yeah... I was—I mean, I will. I just—"

"You won't make it in the team if you don't work hard, Danny. We've had this conversation before."

Daniel let out a frustrated and defeated sigh, not wanting to admit his dad was right but also not knowing what to say. He really just wanted to finish the mystery novel he'd been reading.

Later, as he got on the school bus, he waved bye to his parents, already trying to come up with a plan to avoid coach Reynolds' annoying demands without getting in trouble.

He was just outside the gym when his friend Charlie greeted him. "What's up, Dan? Ready for dodgeball today?"

"Dodgeball...?" Daniel repeated, a smirk slowly forming across his face.

"I know, it's great! I *love* dodgeball, don't you?" Charlie asked absent-mindedly, walking into the gym.

"Oh, yes, I love dodgeball," Daniel replied, now beaming with satisfaction. He looked at coach Reynolds and added, "I sure hope I don't get taken out right away."

Charlie looked at him, confused.

"Are you kidding? I've seen you play before. You're a beast! If we get on the same team, we'll win for sure!"

Daniel felt a slight pang of guilt in his stomach as he saw Charlie's genuine excitement, knowing what he was about to do. Once the teams had been chosen, coach Reynolds made his last announcements before the match.

"Alright everyone, let's have a nice, clean game. And remember to come get your participation slip from me once the game is over. Mrs. Peterson won't let anyone in her 2nd period class who doesn't have the slip!"

"Look," Charlie pointed at the other team, "they've got Kevin *and* Steven. This is going to be a piece of cake," Charlie winked at Daniel, and coach Reynolds blew his whistle to start the match.

At first, Daniel was enjoying himself, throwing and dodging flawlessly much to his teammates' amusement. He was about to throw another shot when he felt slightly out of breath, a stitch forming in his right side. Wiping the sweat off his brow, he decided now was the time to put his plan into action. He tossed an easy shot, lobbing it up higher than normal and allowing Steven, his opponent, to effortlessly catch the ball.

A frowning coach Reynolds blew a quick chirp, signifying Daniel's elimination.

"Oops," he said. Charlie and his teammates all looked confused as Daniel slowly walked to the table to get his participation slip when coach Reynolds abruptly slammed his hairy hand on top of it.

"Nice try, Fisher. I know you did that on purpose."

"Did what on purpose?" Daniel feigned ignorance.

"You threw it, literally. You didn't want to play, so you let Steven catch your throw to get yourself disqualified."

"No! I... why would I...?" He started, but Reynolds' unflinching expression was enough for him to know there was no point in arguing. Daniel cursed himself for making his plan too obvious. "Well, how am I supposed to go to Spanish without the slip, then?"

"Mrs. Peterson will be teaching an extra 7th period after school today, which *you* will be attending. You can spend 2nd period with me, helping me clean up and such. This has been a trend with you lately, Fisher, and it's stopping here."

"But I—"

"You know, I'm not sure why you've been like this. Just a few minutes ago you seemed to be having a good time. If you think you're making the soccer team with this attitude, you're about to be disappointed."

"I... I just got tired."

"Well, you'll have plenty of time to rest now until 3rd period." Coach Reynolds flashed one final disappointed look at Daniel before walking back to the ongoing match.

CHAPTER 2
STRAIGHT-A STUDENT

By the time 3rd period came around, Daniel was exhausted with pure boredom. He'd been sitting in the corner of the gym for what felt like hours. He couldn't believe he was actually excited to sit through Spanish class, his least favorite.

"So, what was that about? Why'd you throw the game?" Charlie asked, sitting himself behind Daniel's seat. The latter shrugged and decided to ignore the question.

"Did we have Spanish homework due—"

"Good morning!" Mr. Roberts interrupted. "Everyone, take out your homework and bring it up to my desk, please."

"We had to write three paragraphs about our favorite foods. Did you forget?" Charlie whispered quietly.

"Oh, great. More trouble for me today," Daniel groaned.

Mr. Roberts waited for the sounds of zipping book bags,

screeching chair legs, shuffling of feet, and quiet chattering as everyone dropped off their worksheets onto his desk. He noticed that Daniel was the only one who didn't get up from his seat.

"I'd like to remind everyone," he said, his glance lingering upon Daniel only slightly longer than the rest of the class, "your homework will count for *thirty-three percent* of your grade. That means *one third*, for those of you skipping Mrs. Peterson's class."

Daniel rolled his eyes, annoyed with himself for having forgotten his homework twice already this month. His good grades streak was at risk. But it wasn't his fault, he told himself. Why did Mr. Roberts have to assign homework on a Friday? *That shouldn't be allowed*, he thought.

After class, he went off to lunch with Charlie, waiting in line at the cafeteria when he saw her. The beautiful Jenny from the advanced honors program.

"There she is," he whispered to Charlie, elbowing his stomach.

"Ouch! Who...?"

"Jenny, obviously. If I make the soccer team *and* get straight A's, she'll definitely go out with me."

Charlie looked puzzled. "You think so? Everyone's saying she's actually been struggling with her grades this year."

"She got sick for one week, it's normal to be a bit behind," Daniel protested, not even sure why. He looked at her again before looking away, as if she were a bright light that he couldn't look at for too long.

CHAPTER 3
MR. DENT'S

After attending Mrs. Peterson's extra 7th period algebra class after normal school hours, per Coach's orders, Daniel left the school. It felt weird to walk home without Charlie next to him. *I wonder if Charlie stopped by Mr. Dent's candy shop today*, he thought.

"Welcome, Daniel! What can I get you today?" Mr. Dent asked as Daniel stopped by, hearing the door chime.

"Good afternoon, Mr. Dent," Daniel said politely. He noticed Mr. Dent still hadn't hung up the top hat he'd started wearing recently. Though it paired well with his painter's brush moustache, Daniel found it to be *over the top*. "May I please have 2 caramel cookie bars?" he finally asked, deciding to keep the joke to himself.

"Absolutely! Coming right up."

Daniel looked around the shop, taking in the powerful sweet aromas and colorful displays. It was honestly quite an impressive shop; there was no other place like it that he knew of. Towers of candy canes and mountains of jawbreakers inside glass boxes, cotton candy hanging from wires like clouds—a sweet-toothed boy's dream.

"Here you go, Daniel. Your total will be five dollars, please," Mr. Dent said as he handed over a neatly hand-wrapped package.

Daniel reached into his pocket and felt his stomach drop as his fingers felt only emptiness. He searched his left pocket. Then, back to his right pocket. Nothing. How could that be? He thought about what he had last spent his money on… and then he remembered. He had come by Mr. Dent's last Friday, spending the last of his cash on cinnamon-sugar popcorn.

Mr. Dent raised an eyebrow. Defeated, Daniel finally answered.

"Sorry, Mr. Dent. I don't have the money. Maybe next time."

He left the shop, cursing his luck today. First, coach Reynolds makes him stay an extra period. Then, he forgets his Spanish homework. And now this?

He kicked a rock on the ground, yelping in pain as the rock was harder than his foot was prepared for, when he heard a strange voice coming from a rosebush on the side of the road.

"Hello, traveler!" Croaked what appeared to be a small orange frog in a cheerful voice.

Daniel's eyes widened.

"Yes, you," the creature added as it hopped off the bush and landed in front of him.

Daniel rubbed his eyes and began walking away, convinced that the stress from this day had left him delirious.

"WAIT—" The frog hopped alongside him as he strode along. Finally, Daniel stopped.

"My name is Finn, and I have a special gift just for you," the frog said with a voice sounding like a sweet melody.

Daniel blinked slowly, remaining cautiously silent. "A frog is talking to me," he said.

"*Toad*, a *toad* is talking to you!" Finn snapped, reaching into a small pouch tied around his neck and pulling out what looked like a small bell. "This bell holds magical powers.

Whenever you ring it, your wishes will come true!" he exclaimed.

Daniel squatted down and, against his better judgment, took the rusty-looking instrument.

"Am I dreaming? What are you?"

"Worry not about me! Make your wishes, of which you have three!"

"Aha! You *just* started rhyming. You weren't rhyming before, which means you're probably in my imagination. My brain is making you up" Daniel said triumphantly, as if he'd solved a puzzle. Yet, to his surprise, Finn reacted nervously, as though he'd been caught.

"I, uh—never mind my rhyming speech! The bell is real... and I'm no... leech?" Daniel glared at him. "Okay, okay. I admit it, I skipped rhyming class at the Magical Toad School. But the bell is real, I promise. I mean, here you are, talking to a toad. That alone should be unbelievable, right?"

"I suppose I can't argue with that. So, I can make three wishes? For anything I want?" He wondered, examining the bell closer.

"Not *anything*, but almost! The exceptions are: you can't wish harm on anyone..."

That's fine, he thought. He wasn't planning on that.

"Nor can you wish for superhuman powers..."

Crud.

"... and lastly, you can't wish for money."

Oh, come on, he thought. Still, Daniel's heart raced with excitement. "Thank you, Mr. Toad—uh, I mean, Mr. Finn!"

"Don't mention it, kid. Now, there are two rules I must mention. First, the wishes take a full day—twenty-four hours—to take effect, so be aware. Secondly—*and you must not forget this,*" he paused, looking up at Daniel with a serious look. "Once you have made your wishes, you will be unable to tell anyone about them."

Daniel was looking at the bell, seemingly distracted.

"Did you hear what I said?"

"What? Yes, of course."

Finn squinted his eyes before continuing. "Now, go on, and choose your wishes wisely! Only a few people have ever had the chance to use the bell, and almost all of them ended up regretting their wishes. If I may recommend it, avoid wishes that are shortcuts for temporary gains."

"Temporary gains?" Daniel asked, looking around to see if anyone had seen him speaking to a toad. But, as he looked down, Finn had vanished.

Wishful Thinking

CHAPTER 4
WISHES

That evening, during dinner with his parents, Daniel eagerly told them about his encounter with Finn and the magical bell. His parents exchanged surprised glances but decided to play along with their son's imagination.

"Alright then, what will you wish for? Hopefully something productive, not some silly selfish thing like 'free candy.'" Mr. Fisher said. Daniel shrugged and said he wasn't sure yet.

He lay in bed that night thinking about what he really wanted. Since he couldn't become rich, or a superhero, he tried thinking about his daily life. What was something practical, something that would really come in handy for him right now?

Well, for starters, he wanted coach Reynolds to stop being such a pain every other morning. His days would always go well if Coach weren't always ruining it, he convinced himself.

"I *wish* coach Reynolds would stop being such a pain" he whispered, ringing the bell softly. But he didn't feel or see anything. Maybe the wish wasn't allowed for some reason?

"Okay then... I *wish* for straight A's in all my classes." This would be perfect, he thought. Jenny would definitely notice him now!

But, again, nothing happened. Had he been tricked? Did he really just imagine Finn, after all? Frustrated, he decided to try an even simpler wish. He remembered his father's words from earlier and figured that would be a good test. Surely there weren't any magical rules against candy, right?

"I *wish* all the candy in Mr. Dent's shop were free!"

And finally, this time, there was a low hum. For a moment, he felt like the air had become charged with electricity, and a purple glow emanated from the bell. He couldn't believe his eyes. It was real!

The bell then vanished in a smoky cloud. *What?* He thought, *does this mean all the other wishes had worked?*

He cursed himself for not taking more time to consider his options... but, hey, it worked! He could barely sleep that night as he considered how much better his life was about to become.

. . .

As Finn had mentioned, the wishes took a full day to take effect, so that by Wednesday he arrived at school ready to experience his new-and-improved coach.

"Morning, everyone!" Coach Reynolds greeted his yawning students. "Today, I've decided you can take a free day."

Daniel smirked knowingly—but dared not tell anyone. It almost felt like, if he told anyone, it would stop working. The coach went on, "There are balls and hula hoops and jumping ropes spread around. Do as you will. No participation slips will be needed today!"

Everyone cheered as their smiling coach walked away to the corner of the gym, staring oddly into the wall without really doing anything.

"Isn't that crazy? Free day!" Daniel said to Charlie.

"Yeah, that's... crazy," Charlie replied, looking at the corner where coach Reynolds was apparently admiring its fascinating cornery-ness. "Well, wanna practice some soccer, then?" He kicked a nearby soccer ball over to Daniel.

"Nah, not today. I'm just going to sit and relax. I can finally get to that mystery book I've been meaning to read."

Charlie looked annoyed. "Suit yourself, Dan. I think you should probably get some practice, though. Tryouts are in a few weeks." But Daniel had already sat down and opened his book.

"I'll be fine, I've practiced enough already," he said, waving a dismissive hand at his friend.

. . .

"Everyone, come on up and get your progress reports for this quarter," Mrs. Peterson announced as her 2nd period class chattered their way inside, motioning to the neat pile stacked on her desk.

"Aw man, a B for Spanish?" Charlie moaned as he sat back down in his seat. "I guess I'll have to study even more for Mr. Roberts' tests."

"Yeah, I guess you should, Charlie," said Daniel, his tone carrying a self-satisfied smugness. "If you do, you'll be able to reach my level," he added, unable to resist bragging as he turned around and flipped over his progress report for Charlie to see, a wide, cocky smile spreading across his face.

"Straight A's??" Charlie protested. "How? You've been slacking on your homework for weeks now!"

"What can I say? Some people are just talented."

Daniel put his progress report away as a puzzled Charlie's chin refused to come back up, his mouth agape with shock. Turning back around with a satisfied sigh, Daniel's thoughts drifted off to his beloved Jenny, thinking of ways to best let her know about his newly discovered mastery of Spanish and math.

. . .

After school, Daniel and Charlie walked home together, talking about their favorite soccer players and making plans for what they'd do once they grew up and joined a pro team.

They walked by Mr. Dent's, and, without skipping a beat, Daniel suggested they go inside.

"But I don't have any mo—"

"It's fine," Daniel said, pulling his friend by his shirt sleeve.

"Daniel, Charlie. Welcome back," Mr. Dent greeted them.

"Hi, Mr. Dent. May I please have ten sour ropes and ten candied apples?"

"Ten? Of *each*?" Charlie asked. "What, so you're rich now, too?"

"Of course not. Look." Daniel pointed at a new sign that had been hung up by the counter:

"ALL ITEMS FREE WHILE SUPPLIES LAST"

"Whoa," Charlie gasped. "Can today get any weirder?" They walked around excitedly and began picking out handfuls of candy and dropping them off on the counter.

"Here you are," said Mr. Dent weakly, a sleepless and stressed look plastered on his face as he handed Daniel the items he'd requested. "Twenty sour ropes and ten candied apples. Oh, and it looks like you've picked out... ten salted caramel bars... two bags of sweet popcorn... six packs of bubblegum... and... four cotton candy rolls." A bead of sweat slid across his forehead as he bagged everything up. "Well, there you go. T-Thank you for coming. Have a nice day, you two."

"Thanks Mr. Dent," both boys replied automatically, grinning widely as they stuffed their faces on their way out.

"How do you figure Mr. Dent can afford that?" asked Charlie as they walked.

"What do you mean?"

"Well, how is he supposed to make money if everything in his store is free?"

"He's a smart man. He probably knows what he's doing," Daniel said, certain that the magic of the bell was handling everything.

As they continued down the path, Daniel saw the same rosebush where he'd first met Finn, but there was no toad or frog anywhere to be found. He did, however, hear what sounded like a sigh coming from the area. *No*, he thought. It was probably just the leaves rustling.

CHAPTER 5
SOCCER

As days passed, Daniel continued to enjoy relaxing and reading during his free P.E. days, which turned out to be *every* P.E. day.

The day of soccer tryouts arrived, and Daniel left for school excited, ready to take the first step in what he saw as a lifelong journey. He had his progress report with him, ready to show it to Ryan Green, the team captain, as proof of his straight A's from coach Reynolds.

Charlie joined him as they walked to the soccer field after school, kicking around an empty can on their way as a warm-up.

"You ready to show Kevin Howard who's boss?" Charlie asked, kicking the can over to Daniel. Kevin, of course, was Daniel's main rival in school, in more ways than one. He'd always enjoyed pushing Daniel's buttons, insulting and annoying him any chance he got.

But, more importantly, he was in the same honors program as Jenny. He took the same classes as her and was often seen with her at lunch and after school.

"Absolutely," Daniel responded, reaching his leg over to catch Charlie's pass and missing only slightly. He readjusted his position and kicked the can back. "Kevin won't make the team even in his wildest dreams."

As they got to the field, they noticed Jenny watching from the bleachers, and she waved and smiled at them. Daniel couldn't believe it. She was being sweet to him!

"Let's go, Daniel!" she said, clapping softly as the boys all lined up in front of Ryan Green. Kevin, positioned at the far end of the line, sneered at Daniel as he lifted up his shiny and expensive cleats.

"Welcome, welcome. Glad to see so many of you could make it," said the captain, looking his prospective members up and down. "As you know, more than half of our team graduated last year, so we have a good number of open positions. I'm not going to make it complicated—we'll just play a quick match and go from there. Any specific questions?"

Once Ryan had answered all questions, they formed two teams and began playing. Daniel felt a rush of confidence every time he looked over at Jenny, who had a seemingly permanent smile on her face.

1 - 0

Charlie scored, and they celebrated quickly before continuing the match. This was turning out to be easier than Daniel had thought. His chemistry with Charlie was proving unstoppable as they predicted their opponents' movements and dribbled around them.

2 - 0

Another goal from Charlie! Jenny cheered on louder now along with a few other girls who had just joined her. Daniel felt a jolt of electricity as he envisioned himself as team captain once Ryan Green graduated.

2 - 1

Kevin Howard scored. Daniel rolled his eyes but tried not to let it bother him too much. Their goalie Mark wasn't playing that well anyway. Kevin had just gotten lucky. He looked back over to Jenny and saw her still smiling encouragingly. He needed to score. He wanted Jenny to see him score.

2 - 2

Kevin Howard scored again. Daniel was now panting as he walked over to his goalie. "Come on! Keep your eye on the ball, Mark."

"You need to be moving faster, Fisher," said a voice behind him. Daniel turned around, ready to fire back an insult at Kevin, but he was met instead with a scowling Ryan Green.

"Oh... yeah, alright," he said awkwardly, bottling up his frustration. He ran back to midfield, trying to keep up with

Charlie's agile pace, but soon found himself completely out of breath. When did Charlie get so fast?

It's fine, he thought. Charlie will be the star forward and Daniel will play a key supporting role. They seem to have good chemistry like this anyway.

At 72 minutes into the match, Charlie made an incredibly difficult pass to Daniel, getting past almost the whole opposing team. Daniel knew he'd have to sprint his lungs out to reach the ball...

3 - 2

He did it! Their team cheered as Daniel gripped his side, feeling a sharp pain stabbing his lungs, but glad nonetheless to have given his all.

4 - 2

Charlie scored their fourth goal with only one minute left, and the game was as good as over. Green blew his whistle, and Charlie high-fived an exhausted Daniel. He could hear Jenny and the girls cheering but he didn't want to look over right now as he gasped for air and wiped the sweat off his eyes.

After a quick water break, Ryan Green announced the time had come.

"Alright everyone, really simple. If I call your name, congratulations! You're in the team. If I don't—you can always try again next season. First up, we have... Charlie! Really excellent job, Charlie."

Daniel gave Charlie a friendly shoulder tap and clapped along with everyone, happy but not surprised that his best friend had made it.

"Next... Mark Stone! Congrats, Mark."

Him? Daniel thought. He figured the other goalie had been much tougher to score on. Maybe it was a sympathy pick?

"Kevin Howard! Nice job, bud."

Oh, great, Daniel thought. Now he'd have to see Kevin's smug face entirely too often.

"...Alan Johnson..."

"…Steven Huggins…"

"…Amir Bell…"

"…and, lastly, Jeff Matthews!"

Daniel felt sick. He felt a lump rushing up his throat. Jenny and Charlie both watched with concern as Daniel disappeared from their sight, rushing off to the nearest restroom.

CHAPTER 6
JENNY

Daniel arrived home exhausted and defeated. Over dinner, he told his parents the bad news.

"I'm sorry, sweetheart. I'm sure you'll make it next year if you try your best," said his mom.

"That's right, son. If it's your dream, it's important to never give up, and to train like your life depends on it. Remember, no cutting corners. I know you can do it," his dad tapped his back with an encouraging smile.

"Thanks," Daniel said weakly to his parents. "I guess I could have trained harder with Charlie."

His mom didn't respond directly. "Did Charlie or Kevin Howard slack off, do you reckon?"

Daniel didn't answer but gave his parents an understanding smile instead. After all, he'd specifically used one of his wishes to have coach Reynolds go easy on him. *What was I thinking*? He thought.

. . .

The following day, when coach Reynolds once again announced a free day, Daniel's mystery book remained in his bag as he decided to go train with Charlie.

When lunchtime came around, he was surprised by Jenny, who approached him herself.

"Hey Dan," she said. "Sorry you didn't make the team. You guys played really well, though!"

"Oh, uh," Daniel choked. Charlie laughed quietly.

"Thanks, Jenny. Yeah, I'm training harder now to make it in next year."

"Good, I'm glad to hear that! So, listen, I heard you've been getting straight A's this year..."

Daniel gulped.

"...including in Spanish. And I was wondering, could you help me out with my Spanish homework? Like, could you maybe tutor me a bit? I've been lagging behind ever since I was sick for that week..."

"I know—I mean, um, yeah I could, definitely!" Daniel said, feeling the familiar sting of regret and anxiety washing over him as he realized he was also behind in his studies. Though, unlike her, he didn't have an excuse. He'd been fully complacent due to his automatic straight A's, courtesy of Finn's magic bell.

"Great! How about we meet at the library after 6th period?" she asked.

"Sounds like a plan, Jen," Daniel winked, his voice surprisingly confident despite his inner panic.

"Wow," Charlie said once Jenny had walked out of earshot, "look at you. Good stuff, man."

"Thanks. Do you have your Spanish textbook with you?"

"Yep, I do. Here you go. Going to do a little warming up beforehand?" Charlie asked.

More like melting up, he thought, scanning the book's table of contents. "Something like that, yeah. Thanks, Charlie."

. . .

He tried to cram as much Spanish as he could for the remaining 20 minutes of lunch, but it was no good. Between the weird new imperfect tense conjugations and the 40 vocabulary terms he'd skipped out on, Daniel was at a loss.

He decided not to dig himself an even deeper hole. He would have to tell Jenny the truth. As 6th period came to a close, his heart was racing as he tried to come up with the right words to tell her. Would she believe him? Should he say the whole truth about the bell, or would that sound completely insane? Would it be better to say he'd just cheated his way into straight A's?

He approached the library feeling his heart in his throat. She was waiting for him inside, seated by a large round table with the Spanish textbook in front of her and last week's worksheets.

"*Hola, Hennifer*," Daniel said, sitting down next to her.

"*Buenas tardes,* Daniel," Jenny smiled softly.

"So, what is it you need help with?"

Jenny looked down at her textbook, which was opened to the chapter on imperfect tense conjugations. "These conjugations... they're so *weird*!"

"I know, aren't they?" Daniel laughed nervously. "To be honest, though—"

"I don't know how you do it, Dan. Even Kevin Howard has been getting B's in our class." Her big hazel eyes studied him. "What's your secret?"

"Flashcards," he said, a little too quickly. "I write the infinitive of the verb on one side, and the conjugation on the other side." He was technically telling the truth—this *was* the method he used to study. He just hadn't done it for the past two chapters.

"Can we do an example?" Jenny asked, pulling out a flashcard from her bookbag. "I'll write an infinitive here," she said, looking through the textbook for an example verb. Having found one, she wrote it on one side of the flashcard.

"Okay, so, I have *mentir*. And now I flip over to the other side and write... what's the imperfect tense of *mentir*?"

It was like God was trying to tell him something. Why did she have to choose the Spanish word for 'to lie'?

"Look, Jenny, the truth is... I don't know. I haven't been studying that much lately."

"What? But you've been getting straight-A's." Jenny's soft expression slowly gave way to a puzzled scowl.

"I know, but... I—I can't say why, but I don't deserve them," he admitted, feeling a wave of relief as he decided to accept God's sign. Jenny opened her mouth to reply, but Daniel already knew what she was going to ask. "I didn't cheat," he said, "at least, not technically."

"Then...?" Jenny was visibly not amused as she waited for an explanation.

"I... I..." Daniel began, but suddenly he felt a burning sensation in his throat and his mouth stopped moving against his will. Then, he remembered.

Once you have made your wishes, you will be unable to tell anyone about them, Finn's voice echoed in his head.

"Sorry, I... I have to go," he managed to say. "The flashcards do work, though, give them a try..." Daniel stood up and walked away, looking for the nearest water fountain to soothe his burning throat. He didn't dare look back at Jenny.

Wishful Thinking

CHAPTER 7
END OF THE LINE

He needed to undo this—undo his wishes. He had to find Finn. *It's the only way out of this mess*, he thought, by now approaching Mr. Dent's candy shop.

He slowed down, out of breath, having been running for ten minutes, when he noticed an enormous sign with red letters in front of the shop's entrance.

"*PERMANENTLY CLOSED*"

No. No way.

"Mr. Dent?" Daniel knocked on the shop's door. Through the glass, he could see a glum and disheveled Mr. Dent packing boxes inside.

The shopkeeper opened the door to a crack, his face partially covered by the door chain. "Hello, Daniel. I'm sorry, but as you can see, we've closed up for good."

"But... why?"

"I... I don't know what happened." He was trembling, almost on the verge of tears. "I don't know why, and I know it makes no sense, but... One day, I decided to stop charging money for my candy. My wife, she... she told me I was crazy, but I didn't listen. I didn't listen. She said I wouldn't be able to afford the rent on this shop if I kept—"

"You... you have to pay rent for this?" Daniel asked, genuinely baffled as a surge of guilt shot up his spine. He'd never considered that Finn's magic bell might not account for things like this.

"Of course!" Tears were now streaming down his face. "Most store owners pay rent, yes. As it stands, I can't even afford to pay my staff. I have no choice. I'm really sorry, Daniel. I need to finish packing now. You... take care of yourself."

Daniel had completely forgotten about the stitch in his lung as an overwhelming sadness took over his body. The sight of Mr. Dent's swollen, crying face as he closed the door was too much. Daniel himself burst into tears, cursing himself for having made such immature and selfish wishes. He walked over to the bush where Finn had first appeared, but he couldn't even utter a single word as he sobbed.

"Daniel, we need to talk," said a strangely melodic yet throaty voice.

"Finn?" he asked, wiping the tears off his face. "Where...?"

"Over here, silly." Finn jumped down from the top of Daniel's head, landing in front of him.

"Oh, thank God, Finn. I need you to help me, please."

"I can tell. It seems you didn't heed my warning. You wished for temporary gains, didn't you?"

"I need to fix it all, Finn. How can I...?"

"Unfortunately, I can't help you. Only you can help yourself now."

"But... I... I didn't know... I didn't think—"

"Self-sacrifice."

"What?"

"To undo the wishes, you need to show that you're willing to give something up—time, energy, quick-and-easy solutions—in other words, only true acts of selflessness can undo acts of selfishness."

Daniel wiped a tear from his cheek as he began to understand.

"Alright, I see..."

"If I may suggest, I believe you can start right here." Finn gestured towards Mr. Dent's shop. Daniel nodded, knowing exactly what to do.

Wishful Thinking

CHAPTER 8
AMENDS

Daniel walked back to Mr. Dents' door and knocked.

"Mr. Dent? It's me again."

"Yes, Daniel, how can I help you?" Mr. Dent's face peered through the barely opened door.

"That's actually what I was going to ask you. I was wondering if there was something I could do to keep you from having to close down. Like, what if I worked here?"

"Daniel, I can't afford rent, let alone—"

"You don't have to pay me. I just want to help. I can even get all my friends to come here and buy your candy."

"Buy?" Mr. Dent said, as if he hadn't heard that word in decades. He opened the door with an obvious hesitation, letting Daniel come inside.

"Yeah, *buy*. Speaking of which, what if I took this..." Daniel took the large **All Items Free** sign and walked to the back of the counter, dropping it in the trash bin. "... And did that?"

It was as though a fog had suddenly lifted from Mr. Dent's eyes. "Yes... Yes, you could definitely do that! Of *course* you could do that! Why, thank you, Daniel!"

There was a low hum in the air, a subtle vibration which Daniel recognized as the same sound Finn's magic bell had made all those days ago.

"You're more than welcome, Mr. Dent. Your candy shop is the best in town, and probably in the world! I'd hate to see it close over a silly mistake." They both smiled at each other and began working, unpacking boxes, and filling up the displays with sweets and, crucially, price tags.

. . .

Daniel! Where have you been? It's way past sundown," said Mrs. Fisher, turning the T.V. off and sneakily slapping her husband's stomach to wake him up.

"I got a job," he replied. "I'm working at Mr. Dent's now."

Mr. Fisher, after composing himself, looked skeptically at Daniel.

"Mr. Dent's? I thought he was shutting down his shop?"

"Exactly," Daniel explained. "I volunteered to help him out for free until the business picks up some steam again."

"And how long did he say that would be?" asked his mom.

"He didn't say, but I have a feeling it won't take long. He had simply forgotten to charge money for his items. Can you *believe* it? That silly, forgetful man." Daniel was smiling, hoping his parents would understand what had happened without him having to say it. After, he quite literally *couldn't* say it.

Mr. and Mrs. Fisher looked at each other, then back at Daniel, not sure what to believe but glad their son was being so kind and generous.

"Well, we'll always support any kind of helping or selfless volunteering you choose to do, Daniel."

"Thanks, dad."

"What about at school? Everything alright?" his mom asked as she sat back down on the couch. Daniel followed suit.

"Yeah, everything is great. There is one thing I wanted your advice on."

"Oh? And what's that?" Mr. Fisher inquired.

"Alright... well, there's this girl, Jenny. She had asked me to help her study. And I told her I would. But, as it turns out, I haven't been paying enough attention in class to actually help her out. Now she's probably really mad at me because I just sort of left her in the library... what should I do?"

"There's a lot to unpack here, Danny..." his mom started.

"Why haven't you been paying attention..." questioned his dad, "...and why did you feel the need to lie to her?" his mom added. Surprisingly, however, neither of them seemed angry, to Daniel's relief.

"I don't really have an excuse," Daniel said, truthfully. "I've been letting myself get lazy and distracted, and I know that's not okay. That's why I want to make things right. And, as for why I lied to her... well, I guess I wanted to impress her after I didn't make it in the soccer team. I know, I know..."

"Daniel, I'm proud of you for being honest," Mrs. Fisher began as her husband nodded in agreement. "I can see that you regret the way you've been acting, and that you want to make amends. That's the mature and righteous thing to do," she added with a smile. "I think Jenny will probably appreciate it if you can be sincerely helpful with her. Just like you volunteered to help Mr. Dent, you can volunteer to help study with her—even if neither one of you knows the material. You can help each other learn."

Daniel nodded. "Let's just hope she doesn't hate my guts."

His dad laughed. "That's a bit of an exaggeration. You're at the age where you might hate country music one week, and the next week you're wearing cowboy boots and learning the fiddle."

They all laughed together, and Daniel thanked them for their help before going to bed.

. . .

"Let me get this straight. *You* want to help me study? After what you did?"

Daniel was sitting across from Jenny at the lunch table. Her girlfriends were whispering and laughing.

"Yeah," he said, ignoring them. "I'm sorry about that. Truth is, I wanted to impress you." He felt his cheeks blush and heard her friends laugh even louder, burying their faces in their hands. "So, if you can forgive me, and study with me, I think it could be good for both of us. I mean, we're both struggling with memorizing our flashcards, so, if we quiz each other out loud, it could help."

Jenny blushed slightly as well, surprised by Daniel's sudden honesty.

"Well, it is true that stacking an auditory component in addition to a visual one can help with information retention," she said, baffling everyone around her. Daniel himself wasn't even sure what she was saying. "Fine," she finally concluded, "But do *not* be late, Daniel Fisher. Four o'clock, sharp."

Daniel Fisher smiled wider than he knew his mouth could stretch, taking great joy in the sudden silence coming from her friends. "Great! *Hasta luego,* then, *Hennifer.*"

Later that day, after they'd spent two hours studying in the library, Daniel heard the magical humming in the air again, signifying another wish being undone. Though he knew he'd have to work for his straight A's again, he felt like yet another weight had been lifted off his shoulders. *Only one more to go.*

. . .

"So, you and Jenny seem to be getting along well, now." Charlie said the next day as they waited in line outside the gym, waiting for coach Reynolds to open the door.

"Yep! She's really smart, too. She said she'll help me with algebra, which... you know how badly I need that."

They both laughed together as they heard the now-familiar sound of coach Reynolds dropping sports balls all over the gym floor coming from the other side of the door.

"Enjoy your free days while you can, slackers," sneered Kevin Howard as he moved up the line, skipping several other students. "*Rumor has it*, Reynolds might be getting canned. Principal Hunter's not too happy with all the free days we've been getting. He won't last another week if he keeps this up. At least, *according to rumor.*"

Charlie rolled his eyes, turning around to confront him.

"Yes, Kevin, we all know your mom is on the school board, and that she tells you all these *rumors* that go around. But, at the end of the day, that's still all they are. Rumors. I mean, she was wrong about the soda vending machines we were supposedly getting, wasn't she?"

Kevin shrugged. "Believe what you will. I, for one, am tired of all these boring free days. Isn't everyone?" He asked the other students in the line, who all reluctantly nodded and hummed in agreement.

Daniel felt uneasy. Kevin seemed much too confident for his liking: normally, he wouldn't shut up until he felt he'd thoroughly convinced them that the '*rumor*' was true. Yet here he was, turning his back on them with total disregard.

Finally, the door opened. "Come on in, kids. We have a free day again today. Enjoy," he said as he began walking away. Then, in an instant, Daniel knew exactly what he had to do.

"Actually, coach Reynolds, I wanted to ask you something," Daniel said as he followed the coach to the corner.

"Sure thing, Daniel. What is it?"

"Well, I was talking with everyone else, and we're kind of tired of all these free days. We were hoping you could, you know… do your thing? Make us run laps, do exercises and stuff? I mean, look at Kevin Howard. He looks like he's been eating tubs of lard with all that weight he's gained recently."

"Does he, now? I hadn't noticed…"

It wasn't working. Coach Reynolds seemed completely uninterested in what Daniel was saying.

"Yes, coach, we need to get back into the flow of things. Please."

"I'm a new man, Fisher. I've learned that in life, we should only do things that are popular with everyone. Please the crowd, ease the crown," he said, pointing at his head.

"I'm not sure that's a good philosophy, coach. What if the crowd decides to burn down a building, walk in the middle of the street, or worse, they decide to throw away the rulebook altogeth—"

"They'd *never*—"

"Sometimes they *do*!" Daniel insisted. "Watch."

Daniel turned to face the rest of the students. "Attention, everyone, I'd like to introduce you to your new P.E. coach: *me*, coach Fisher!"

"What do you think you're doing, Daniel?" The kids laughed as a deep furrow formed in coach Reynolds' brow.

"Now, as your new coach," Daniel continued, ignoring but pleased to see the beginnings of some kind of reaction bubbling up inside his coach, "I want to see a show of hands. Who here is tired of all the free days? Who wants coach Reynolds to be tough again?"

"Daniel, stop..."

The crowd murmured in agreement.

"I said *hands*, please," Daniel continued the act.

Every single hand went up, including the wildcard that was Kevin Howard.

"*Daniel...*"

"See? Look at that!" Daniel said, beaming as he turned around to face his coach. "You may put your hands down now, class."

"*FISHER!* You will STOP impersonating a teacher and/or faculty member this very instant or so *help* me Lord, I will give you two weeks' detention!"

So be it, Daniel thought. He couldn't believe it, but he found himself happily accepting this trade in order to have his old coach back.

"You said pleasing the crowd was your new philosophy, coach. Well, this crowd wants the old you back. Now, if you'll excuse me, I have a class to coach. Everyone! I want to see ten laps around the gym, starting *now!*"

"That's it," said coach Reynolds, stomping over to his table filling out a detention slip. As he did so, Daniel heard the final hum of Finn's bell.

"There you go, wise guy. Two weeks' detention, as promised. And as for *you*," he looked at the other students, "I don't know why you're not running yet. You have fifteen laps to go."

"*Fifteen*?" Kevin Howard moaned. "But—"

"Make that twenty for you, Howard."

Daniel bowed to the class, humbly and victoriously accepting his (and Kevin's) punishment as a sigh of relief and satisfaction rolled out of his smiling mouth.

He could barely sleep that night as he considered how much better his life was about to become.

. . .

Somewhere in the distance, an orange toad hopped into an open semi, his work in Riverdale finished.